'THEY DIDN'T SEEM TO TAKE MUCH INTEREST IN MY PRIVATE PARTS WHICH TO TELL THE TRUTH WERE NOTHING TO WRITE HOME ABOUT.'

SAMUEL BECKETT
Born 1906, Dublin, Ireland
Died 1989, Paris, France

La Fin and *Le Calmant* were first published in the original
French in 1954 in *Nouvelles et Textes pour rien*. In 1967 they were
translated into English and published as *Stories and Texts for
Nothing*. Beckett translated 'The Calmative' and Richard Seaver
translated 'The End' in collaboration with Beckett.

BECKETT IN PENGUIN MODERN CLASSICS
First Love and Other Novellas

Contents

The End

They clothed me and gave me money. I knew what the money was for, it was to get me started. When it was gone I would have to get more, if I wanted to go on. The same for the shoes, when they were worn out I would have to get them mended, or get myself another pair, or go on barefoot, if I wanted to go on. The same for the coat and trousers, needless to say, with this difference, that I could go on in my shirtsleeves, if I wanted. The clothes – shoes, socks, trousers, shirt, coat, hat – were not new, but the deceased must have been about my size. That is to say, he must have been a little shorter, a little thinner, for the clothes did not fit me so well in the beginning as they did at the end, the shirt especially, and it was many a long day before I could button it at the neck, or profit by the collar that went with it, or pin the tails together between my legs in the way my mother had taught me. He must have put on his Sunday best to go to the consultation, perhaps for the first time, unable to bear it any longer. Be that as it may the hat was a bowler, in good shape.

I said, Keep your hat and give me back mine. I added, Give me back my greatcoat. They replied that they had burnt them, together with my other clothes. I understood then that the end was near, at least fairly near. Later on I tried to exchange this hat for a cap, or a slouch which could be pulled down over my face, but without much success. And yet I could not go about bare-headed, with my skull in the state it was. At first this hat was too small, then it got used to me. They gave me a tie, after long discussion. It seemed a pretty tie to me, but I didn't like it. When it came at last I was too tired to send it back. But in the end it came in useful. It was blue, with kinds of little stars. I didn't feel well, but they told me I was well enough. They didn't say in so many words that I was as well as I would ever be, but that was the implication. I lay inert on the bed and it took three women to put on my trousers. They didn't seem to take much interest in my private parts which to tell the truth were nothing to write home about, I didn't take much interest in them myself. But they might have passed some remark. When they had finished I got up and finished dressing unaided. They told me to sit on the bed and wait. All the bedding had disappeared. It made me angry that they had not let me wait in the familiar bed, instead of leaving me standing in the cold, in these clothes that smelt of sulphur. I said, You might have left me in the bed till the last moment. Men all in white came in with mallets in their hands. They dismantled the bed and took away the pieces. One of the women followed them out and came back with a chair which she set before me. I had done well to pretend I was angry. But to make it quite clear to them how angry I was that they had not left me in my bed I gave the chair a kick that sent it flying. A man came in and made a sign to me to follow him. In the hall he gave me a paper to sign. What's this, I said, a safe-conduct? It's a receipt, he said for the clothes and money you have received. What money? I said. It was then I received the money. To think I had almost departed without a penny in my pocket. The sum was not large, compared to other sums, but to me it seemed large. I saw the familiar objects, companions of so many bearable hours. The stool, for example, dearest of all. The long afternoons together, waiting for it to be time for bed. At times I felt its wooden life invade me, till I myself became a piece of old wood. There was even a hole for my cyst. Then the window pane with the patch of frosting gone, where I used to press my eye in the hour of need, and rarely in vain. I am greatly obliged to you, I said, is there a law which prevents you from throwing me out naked and penniless? That would damage our reputation in the long run, he replied. Could they not possibly keep me a little longer, I said, I could make myself useful.

Useful, he said, joking apart you would be willing to make yourself useful? A moment later he went on, If they believed you were really willing to make yourself useful they would keep you, I am sure. The number of times I had said I was going to make myself useful, I wasn't going to start that again. How weak I felt! Perhaps, I said, they would consent to take back the money and keep me a little longer. This is a charitable institution, he said, and the money is a gift you receive when you leave. When it is gone you will have to get more, if you want to go on. Never come back here whatever you do, you would not be let in. Don't go to any of our branches either, they would turn you away. Exelmans! I cried. Come come, he said, and anyway no one understands a tenth of what you say. I'm so old, I said. You are not so old as all that, he said. May I stay here just a little longer, I said, till the rain is over? You may wait in the cloister, he said, the rain will go on all day. You may wait in the cloister till six o'clock, you will hear the bell. If anyone challenges you, you need only say you have permission to shelter in the cloister. Whose name will I give? I said. Weir, he said.

I had not been long in the cloister when the rain stopped and the sun came out. It was low and I reckoned it must be getting on for six, considering the season. I stayed there looking through the archway at the sun as it went down behind the cloister. A man appeared and asked me what I was doing. What do you want? were the words he used. Very friendly. I replied that I had Mr Weir's permission to stay in the cloister till six o'clock. He went away, but came back immediately. He must have spoken to Mr Weir in the interim, for he said, You must not loiter in the cloister now the rain is over.

Now I was making my way through the garden. There was that strange light which follows a day of persistent rain, when the sun comes out and the sky clears too late to be of any use. The earth makes a sound as of sighs and the last drops fall from the emptied cloudless sky. A small boy, stretching out his hands and looking up at the blue sky, asked his mother how such a thing was possible. Fuck off, she said. I suddenly remembered I had not thought of asking Mr Weir for a piece of bread. He would surely have given it to me. I had as a matter of fact thought of it during our conversation in the hall, I had said to myself, Let us first finish our conversation, then I'll ask. I knew well they would not keep me. I would gladly have turned back, but I was afraid one of the guards would stop me and tell me I would never see Mr Weir again. That might have added to my sorrow. And anyway I never turned back on such occasions.

In the street I was lost. I had not set foot in this part of the city for a long time and it seemed greatly changed.

Whole buildings had disappeared, the palings had changed position, and on all sides I saw, in great letters, the names of tradesmen I had never seen before and would have been at a loss to pronounce. There were streets where I remembered none, some I did remember had vanished and others had completely changed their names. The general impression was the same as before. It is true I did not know the city very well. Perhaps it was quite a different one. I did not know where I was supposed to be going. I had the great good fortune, more than once, not to be run over. My appearance still made people laugh, with that hearty jovial laugh so good for the health. By keeping the red part of the sky as much as possible on my right hand I came at last to the river. Here all seemed at first sight more or less as I had left it. But if I had looked more closely I would doubtless have discovered many changes. And indeed I subsequently did so. But the general appearance of the river, flowing between its quays and under its bridges, had not changed. Yes, the river still gave the impression it was flowing in the wrong direction. That's all a pack of lies I feel. My bench was still there. It was shaped to fit the curves of the seated body. It stood beside a watering trough, gift of a Mrs Maxwell to the city horses, according to the inscription. During the short time I rested there several horses took advantage of this monument. The iron shoes approached and the jingle of the harness. Then silence. That was the horse looking at me. Then the noise of pebbles and mud that horses make when drinking. Then the silence again. That was the horse looking at me again. Then the pebbles again. Then the silence again. Till the horse had finished drinking or the driver deemed it had drunk its fill. The horses were uneasy. Once, when the noise stopped, I turned and saw the horse looking at me. The driver too was looking at me. Mrs Maxwell would have been pleased if she could have seen her trough rendering such services to the city horses. When it was night, after a tedious twilight, I took off my hat which was paining me. I longed to be under cover again, in an empty place, close and warm, with artificial light, an oil lamp for choice, with a pink shade for preference. From time to time someone would come to make sure I was all right and needed nothing. It was long since I had longed for anything and the effect on me was horrible.

In the days that followed I visited several lodgings, without much success. They usually slammed the door in my face, even when I showed my money and offered to pay a week in advance, or even two. It was in vain I put on my best manners, smiled and spoke distinctly, they slammed the door in my face before I could even finish my little speech. It was at this time I perfected a method of doffing my hat at once courteous and discreet, neither servile nor insolent. I slipped it smartly forward, held it a second poised in such a way that the person addressed could not see my skull, then slipped it back. To do that naturally, without creating an unfavourable impression, is no easy matter. When I deemed that to tip my hat would suffice, I naturally did no more than tip it. But to tip one's hat is no easy matter either. I subsequently solved this problem, always fundamental in time of adversity, by wearing a kepi and saluting in military fashion, no, that must be wrong, I don't know, I had my hat at the end. I never made the mistake of wearing medals. Some landladies were in such need of money that they let me in immediately and showed me the room. But I couldn't come to an agreement with any of them. Finally I found a basement. With this woman I came to an agreement at once. My oddities, that's the expression she used, did not alarm her. She nevertheless insisted on making the bed and cleaning the room once a week, instead of once a month as I requested. She told me that while she was cleaning, which would not take long, I could wait in the area. She added, with a great deal of feeling, that she would never put me out in bad weather. This woman was Greek, I think, or Turkish. She never spoke about herself. I somehow got the idea she was a widow or at least that her husband had left her.

She had a strange accent. But so had I with my way of assimilating the vowels and omitting the consonants.

Now I didn't know where I was. I had a vague vision, not a real vision, I didn't see anything, of a big house five or six stories high, one of a block perhaps. It was dusk when I got there and I did not pay the same heed to my surroundings as I might have done if I had suspected they were to close about me. And by then I must have lost all hope. It is true that when I left this house it was a glorious day, but I never look back when leaving. I must have read somewhere, when I was small and still read, that it is better not to look back when leaving. And yet I sometimes did. But even without looking back it seems to me I should have seen something when leaving. But there it is. All I remember is my feet emerging from my shadow, one after the other. My shoes had stiffened and the sun brought out the cracks in the leather.

I was comfortable enough in this house, I must say. Apart from a few rats I was alone in the basement. The woman did her best to respect our agreement. About noon she brought me a big tray of food and took away the tray of the previous day. At the same time she brought me a clean chamber-pot. The chamber-pot had a large handle which she slipped over her arm, so that both her hands were free to carry the tray. The rest of the day I saw no more of her except sometimes when she peeped in to make sure nothing had happened to me. Fortunately I did not need affection. From my bed I saw the feet coming and going on the sidewalk. Certain evenings, when the weather was fine and I felt equal to it, I fetched my chair into the area and sat looking up into the skirts of the women passing by. Once I sent for a crocus bulb and planted it in the dark area, in an old pot. It must have been coming up to spring, it was probably not the right time for it. I left the pot outside, attached to a string I passed through the window. In the evening, when the weather was fine, a little light crept up the wall. Then I sat down beside the window and pulled on the string to keep the pot in the light and warmth. That can't have been easy, I don't see how I managed it. It was probably not the right thing for it. I manured it as best I could and pissed on it when the weather was dry. It may not have been the right thing for it. It sprouted, but never any flowers, just a wilting stem and a few chlorotic leaves. I would have liked to have a yellow crocus, or a hyacinth, but there, it was not to be. She wanted to take it away, but I told her to leave it. She wanted to buy me another, but I told her I didn't want another. What lacerated me most was the din of the newspaper boys. They went pounding by every day at the same hours, their heels thudding on the sidewalk, crying the names of their papers and even the headlines. The house noises disturbed me less. A little girl, unless it was a little boy, sang every evening at the same hour, somewhere above me. For a long time I could not catch the words. But hearing them day after day I finally managed to catch a few. Strange words for a little girl, or a little boy. Was it a song in my head or did it merely come from without? It was a sort of lullaby, I believe. It often sent me to sleep, even me. Sometimes it was a little girl who came. She had long red hair hanging down in two braids. I didn't know who she was. She lingered awhile in the room, then went away without a word. One day I had a visit from a policeman. He said I had to be watched, without explaining why. Suspicious, that was it, he told me I was suspicious. I let him talk. He didn't dare arrest me. Or perhaps he had a kind heart. A priest too, one day I had a visit from a priest. I informed him I belonged to a branch of the reformed church. He asked me what kind of clergyman I would like to see. Yes, there's that about the reformed church, you're lost, it's unavoidable. Perhaps he had a kind heart. He told me to let him know if I needed a helping hand. A helping hand! He gave me his name and explained where I could reach him. I should have made a note of it.

One day the woman made me an offer. She said she was in urgent need of cash and that if I could pay her six months in advance she would reduce my rent by one fourth during that period, something of that kind. This had the advantage of saving six weeks' (?) rent and the disadvantage of almost exhausting my small capital. But could you call that a disadvantage? Wouldn't I stay on in any case till my last penny was gone, and even longer, till she put me out? I gave her the money and she gave me a receipt.

One morning, not long after this transaction, I was awakened by a man shaking my shoulder. It could not have been much past eleven. He requested me to get up and leave his house immediately. He was most correct, I must say. His surprise, he said, was no less than mine. It was his house. His property. The Turkish woman had left the day before. But I saw her last night, I said. You must be mistaken, he said, for she brought the keys to my office no later than yesterday afternoon. But I just paid her six months' rent in advance, I said. Get a refund, he said. But I don't even know her name, I said, let alone her address. You don't know her name? he said. He must have thought I was lying. I'm sick, I said, I can't leave like this, without any notice. You're not so sick as all that, he said. He offered to send for a taxi, even an ambulance if I preferred. He said he needed the room immediately for his pig which even as he spoke was catching cold in a cart before the door and no one to look after him but a stray urchin whom he had never set eyes on before and who was probably busy tormenting him. I asked if he couldn't let me have another place, any old corner where I could lie down long enough to recover from the shock and decide what to do. He said he could not. Don't think I'm being unkind, he added. I could live here with the pig, I said, I'd look after him. The long months of peace, wiped out in an instant! Come now, come now, he said, get a grip on yourself, be a man, get up, that's enough. After all it was no concern of his. He had really been most patient. He must have visited the basement while I was sleeping.

I felt weak. Perhaps I was. I stumbled in the blinding light. A bus took me into the country. I sat down in a field in the sun. But it seems to me that was much later. I stuck leaves under my hat, all the way round, to make a shade. The night was cold. I wandered for hours in the fields. At last I found a heap of dung. The next day I started back to the city. They made me get off three buses. I sat down by the roadside and dried my clothes in the sun. I enjoyed doing that. I said to myself, There's nothing more to be done now, not a thing, till they are dry. When they were dry I brushed them with a brush, I think a kind of curry comb, that I found in a stable. Stables have always been my salvation. Then I went to the house and begged a glass of milk and a slice of bread and butter. They gave me everything except the butter.

May I rest in the stable? I said. No, they said. I still stank, but with a stink that pleased me. I much preferred it to my own which moreover it prevented me from smelling, except a waft now and then. In the days that followed I took the necessary steps to recover my money. I don't know exactly what happened, whether I couldn't find the address, or whether there was no such address, or whether the Greek woman was unknown there. I ransacked my pockets for the receipt, to try and decipher the name. It wasn't there. Perhaps she had taken it back while I was sleeping. I don't know how long I wandered thus, resting now in one place, now in another, in the city and in the country. The city had suffered many changes. Nor was the country as I remembered it. The general effect was the same. One day I caught sight of my son. He was striding along with a briefcase under his arm. He took off his hat and bowed and I saw he was as bald as a coot. I was almost certain it was he. I turned round to gaze after him. He went bustling along on his duck feet, bowing and scraping and flourishing his hat left and right. The insufferable son of a bitch.

One day I met a man I had known in former times. He lived in a cave by the sea. He had an ass that grazed winter and summer, over the cliffs, or along the little tracks leading down to the sea. When the weather was very bad this ass came down to the cave of his own

accord and sheltered there till the storm was past. So
they had spent many a night huddled together, while the
wind howled and the sea pounded on the shore. With
the help of this ass he could deliver sand, sea-wrack and
shells to the townsfolk, for their gardens. He couldn't
carry much at a time, for the ass was old and small and
the town was far. But in this way he earned a little money,
enough to keep him in tobacco and matches and to buy
a piece of bread from time to time. It was during one of
these excursions that he met me, in the suburbs. He was
delighted to see me, poor man. He begged me to go
home with him and spend the night. Stay as long as you
like, he said. What's wrong with your ass? I said. Don't
mind him, he said, he doesn't know you. I reminded him
that I wasn't in the habit of staying more than two or
three minutes with anyone and that the sea did not agree
with me. He seemed deeply grieved to hear it. So you
won't come, he said. But to my amazement I got up on
the ass and off we went, in the shade of the red chestnuts
springing from the sidewalk. I held the ass by the mane,
one hand in front of the other. The little boys jeered and
threw stones, but their aim was poor, for they only hit
me once, on the hat. A policeman stopped us and accused
us of disturbing the peace. My friend replied that we
were as nature had made us, the boys too were as
nature had made them. It was inevitable, under these

conditions, that the peace should be disturbed from time to time. Let us continue on our way, he said, and order will soon be restored throughout your beat. We followed the quiet, dust-white inland roads with their hedges of hawthorn and fuchsia and their footpaths fringed with wild grass and daisies. Night fell. The ass carried me right to the mouth of the cave, for in the dark I could not have found my way down the path winding steeply to the sea. Then he climbed back to his pasture.

I don't know how long I stayed there. The cave was nicely arranged, I must say. I treated my crablice with saltwater and seaweed, but a lot of nits must have survived. I put compresses of seaweed on my skull, which gave me great relief, but not for long. I lay in the cave and sometimes looked out at the horizon. I saw above me a vast trembling expanse without islands or promontories. At night a light shone into the cave at regular intervals. It was here I found the phial in my pocket. It was not broken, for the glass was not real glass. I thought Mr Weir had confiscated all my belongings. My host was out most of the time. He fed me on fish. It is easy for a man, a proper man, to live in a cave, far from everybody. He invited me to stay as long as I liked. If I preferred to be alone he would gladly prepare another cave for me further on. He would bring me food every day and drop in from time to time to make sure I was all right and

needed nothing. He was kind. Unfortunately I did not
need kindness. You wouldn't know of a lake dwelling?
I said. I couldn't bear the sea, its splashing and heaving,
its tides and general convulsiveness. The wind at least
sometimes stops. My hands and feet felt as though they
were full of ants. This kept me awake for hours on end.
If I stayed here something awful would happen to me, I
said, and a lot of good that would do me. You'd get
drowned, he said. Yes, I said, or jump off the cliff. And
to think I couldn't live anywhere else, he said, in my
cabin in the mountains I was wretched. Your cabin in the
mountains? I said. He repeated the story of his cabin in
the mountains, I had forgotten it, it was as though I were
hearing it for the first time. I asked him if he still had it.
He replied he had not seen it since the day he fled from
it, but that he believed it was still there, a little decayed
no doubt. But when he urged me to take the key
I refused, saying I had other plans. You will always find
me here, he said, if you ever need me. Ah people. He
gave me his knife.

What he called his cabin in the mountains was a sort
of wooden shed. The door had been removed, for fire-
wood, or for some other purpose. The glass had disappeared from the window. The roof had fallen in at
several places. The interior was divided, by the remains
of a partition, into two unequal parts. If there had been

any furniture it was gone. The vilest acts had been committed on the ground and against the walls. The floor was strewn with excrements, both human and animal, with condoms and vomit. In a cowpat a heart had been traced, pierced by an arrow. And yet there was nothing to attract tourists. I noticed the remains of abandoned nosegays. They had been greedily gathered, carried for miles, then thrown away, because they were cumbersome or already withered. This was the dwelling to which I had been offered the key.

The scene was the familiar one of grandeur and desolation.

Nevertheless it was a roof over my head. I rested on a bed of ferns, gathered at great labour with my own hands. One day I couldn't get up. The cow saved me. Goaded by the icy mist she came in search of shelter. It was probably not the first time. She can't have seen me. I tried to suck her, without much success. Her udder was covered with dung. I took off my hat and, summoning all my energy, began to milk her into it. The milk fell to the ground and was lost, but I said to myself, No matter, it's free. She dragged me across the floor, stopping from time to time only to kick me. I didn't know our cows too could be so inhuman. She must have recently been milked. Clutching the dug with one hand I kept my hat under it with the other. But in the end she prevailed. For she dragged me across the threshold and out into the giant streaming ferns, where I was forced to let go.

As I drank the milk I reproached myself with what I had done. I could no longer count on this cow and she would warn the others. More master of myself I might have made a friend of her. She would have come every day, perhaps accompanied by other cows. I might have learnt to make butter, even cheese. But I said to myself, No, all is for the best.

Once on the road it was all downhill. Soon there were carts, but they all refused to take me up. In other clothes, with another face, they might have taken me up. I must have changed since my expulsion from the basement. The face notably seemed to have attained its climacteric. The humble, ingenuous smile would no longer come, nor the expression of candid misery, showing the stars and the distaff. I summoned them, but they would not come. A mask of dirty old hairy leather, with two holes and a slit, it was too far gone for the old trick of please your honour and God reward you and pity upon me. It was disastrous. What would I crawl with in future? I lay down on the side of the road and began to writhe each time I heard a cart approaching. That was so they would not think I was sleeping or resting. I tried to groan, Help! Help! But the tone that came out was that of polite conversation. My hour was not yet come and I could no longer groan. The last time I had cause to groan I had groaned as well as ever, and no heart within miles of me to melt. What was to become of me? I said to myself, I'll learn again. I lay down across the road at a narrow place, so that the carts could not pass without passing over my body, with one wheel at least, or two if there were four. But the day came when, looking round me, I was in the suburbs, and from there to the old haunts it was not far, beyond the stupid hope of rest or less pain.

So I covered the lower part of my face with a black rag and went and begged at a sunny corner. For it seemed to me my eyes were not completely spent, thanks perhaps to the dark glasses my tutor had given me. He had given me the *Ethics* of Geulincx. They were a man's glasses, I was a child. They found him dead, crumpled up in the water closet, his clothes in awful disorder, struck down by an infarctus. Ah what peace. The *Ethics* had his name (Ward) on the flyleaf, the glasses had belonged to him. The bridge, at the time I am speaking of, was of brass wire, of the kind used to hang pictures and big mirrors, and two long black ribbons served as wings. I wound them round my ears and then down under my chin where I tied them together. The lenses had suffered, from rubbing in my pocket against each other and against the other objects there. I thought Mr Weir had confiscated all my belongings. But I had no further need of these glasses and used them merely to soften the glare of the sun. I should never have mentioned them. The rag gave me a lot of trouble. I got it in the end from the lining of my greatcoat, no, I had no greatcoat now, of my coat then. The result was a grey rag rather than a black, perhaps even chequered, but I had to make do with it. Till afternoon I held my face raised towards the southern sky, then towards the western till night. The bowl gave me a lot of trouble. I couldn't use my hat because of my skull. As for holding out my hand, that was quite out of the question. So I got a tin and hung it from a button of my greatcoat, what's the matter with me, of my coat, at pubis level. It did not hang plumb, it leaned respectfully towards the passer-by, he had only to drop his mite. But that obliged him to come up close to me, he was in danger of touching me. In the end I got a bigger tin, a kind of big tin box, and I placed it on the sidewalk at my feet. But people who give alms don't much care to toss them, there's something contemptuous about this gesture which is repugnant to sensitive natures. To say nothing of their having to aim. They are prepared to give, but not for their gift to go rolling under the passing feet or under the passing wheels, to be picked up perhaps by some undeserving person. So they don't give. There are those, to be sure, who stoop, but generally speaking people who give alms don't much care to stoop. What they like above all is to sight the wretch from afar, get ready their penny, drop it in their stride and hear the God bless you dying away in the distance. Personally I never said that, nor anything like it, I wasn't much of a believer, but I did make a noise with my mouth. In the end I got a kind of board or tray and tied it to my neck and waist. It jutted out just at the right height, pocket height, and its edge was far enough from my person for the coin to be bestowed without danger. Some days I strewed it with flowers, petals, buds and that herb which men call fleabane, I believe, in a word whatever I could find. I didn't go out of my way to look for them, but all the pretty things of this description that came my way were for the board. They must have thought I loved nature. Most of the time I looked up at the sky, but without focusing it, for why focus it? Most of the time it was a mixture of white, blue and grey, and then at evening all the evening colours. I felt it weighing softly on my face, I rubbed my face against it, one cheek after the other, turning my head from side to side. Now and then to rest my neck I dropped my head on my chest. Then I could see the board in the distance, a haze of many colours. I leaned against the wall, but without nonchalance, I shifted my weight from one foot to the other and my hands clutched the lapels of my coat. To beg with your hands in your pockets makes a bad impression, it irritates the workers, especially in winter. You should never wear gloves either. There were guttersnipes who swept away all I had earned, under cover of giving me a coin. It was to buy sweets. I unbuttoned my trousers discreetly to scratch myself. I scratched myself in an upward direction, with four nails. I pulled on the hairs, to get relief. It passed the time, time flew when I scratched myself. Real scratching is superior to masturbation, in my opinion. One can masturbate up to the age of seventy, and even beyond, but in the end it becomes a mere habit. Whereas to scratch myself properly I would have needed a dozen hands. I itched all over, on the privates, in the bush up to the navel, under the arms, in the arse, and then patches of eczema and psoriasis that I could set raging merely by thinking of them. It was in the arse I had the most pleasure, I stuck in my forefinger up to the knuckle. Later, if I had to shit, the pain was atrocious. But I hardly shat any more. Now and then a flying machine flew by, sluggishly it seemed to me. Often at the end of the day I discovered the legs of my trousers all wet. That must have been the dogs. I personally pissed very little. If by chance the need came on me a little squirt in my fly was enough to relieve it. Once at my post I did not leave it till nightfall. I had no appetite, God tempered the wind to me. After work I bought a bottle of milk and drank it in the evening in the shed. Better still, I got a little boy to buy it for me, always the same, they wouldn't serve me,

I don't know why. I gave him a penny for his pains. One day I witnessed a strange scene. Normally I didn't see a great deal. I didn't hear a great deal either. I didn't pay attention. Strictly speaking I wasn't there. Strictly speaking I believe I've never been anywhere. But that day I must have come back. For some time past a sound had been scarifying me. I did not investigate the cause, for I said to myself, It's going to stop. But as it did not stop I had no choice but to find out the cause. It was a man perched on the roof of a car and haranguing the passersby. That at least was my interpretation. He was bellowing so loud that snatches of his discourse reached my ears. Union . . . brothers . . . Marx . . . capital . . . bread and butter . . . love. It was all Greek to me. The car was drawn up against the kerb, just in front of me, I saw the orator from behind. All of a sudden he turned and pointed at me, as at an exhibit. Look at this down and out, he vociferated, this leftover. If he doesn't go down on all fours, it's for fear of being impounded. Old, lousy, rotten, ripe for the muckheap. And there are a thousand like him, worse than him, ten thousand, twenty thousand –. A voice, Thirty thousand. Every day you pass them by, resumed the orator, and when you have backed a winner you fling them a farthing. Do you ever think? The voice, God forbid. A penny, resumed the orator, tuppence –. The voice, Thruppence. It never enters your head, resumed the orator, that your charity is a crime, an incentive to slavery, stultification and organized murder. Take a good look at this living corpse. You may say it's his own fault. Ask him if it's his own fault. The voice, Ask him yourself. Then he bent forward and took me to task. I had perfected my board. It now consisted of two boards hinged together, which enabled me, when my work was done, to fold it and carry it under my arm. I liked doing little odd jobs. So I took off the rag, pocketed the few coins I had earned, untied the board, folded it and put it under my arm. Do you hear me, you crucified bastard! cried the orator. Then I went away, although it was still light. But generally speaking it was a quiet corner, busy but not overcrowded, thriving and well-frequented. He must have been a religious fanatic, I could find no other explanation. Perhaps he was an escaped lunatic. He had a nice face, a little on the red side.

I did not work every day. I had practically no expenses. I even managed to put a little aside, for my very last days. The days I did not work I spent lying in the shed. The shed was on a private estate, or what had once been a private estate, on the riverside. This estate, the main entrance to which opened on a narrow, dark and silent street, was enclosed with a wall, except of course on the river front, which marked its northern boundary for a distance of about thirty yards. From the last quays beyond the water the eyes rose to a confusion of low houses, wasteland, hoardings, chimneys, steeples and towers. A kind of parade ground was also to be seen, where soldiers played football all the year round. Only the ground-floor windows – no, I can't. The estate seemed abandoned. The gates were locked and the paths overgrown with grass. Only the ground-floor windows had shutters. The others were sometimes lit at night, faintly, now one, now another. At least that was my impression. Perhaps it was reflected light. In this shed, the day I adopted it, I found a boat, upside down. I righted it, chocked it up with stones and pieces of wood, took out the thwarts and made my bed inside. The rats had difficulty in getting at me, because of the bulge of the hull. And yet they longed to. Just think of it, living flesh, for in spite of everything I was still living flesh. I had lived too long among rats, in my chance dwellings, to share the dread they inspire in the vulgar. I even had a soft spot in my heart for them. They came with such confidence towards me, it seemed without the least repugnance. They made their toilet with catlike gestures. Toads at evening, motionless for hours, lap flies from the air. They like to squat where cover ends and open air begins, they favour thresholds. But I had to contend now with water rats, exceptionally lean and ferocious. So I made a kind of lid with stray boards. It's incredible the number of boards I've come across in my lifetime, I never needed a board but there it was, I had only to stoop and pick it up. I liked doing little odd jobs, no, not particularly, I didn't mind. It completely covered the boat, I'm referring again to the lid. I pushed it a little towards the stern, climbed into the boat by the bow, crawled to the stern, raised my feet and pushed the lid back towards the bow till it covered me completely. But what did my feet push against? They pushed against a crossbar I nailed to the lid for that purpose, I liked these little odd jobs. But it was better to climb into the boat by the stern and pull back the lid with my hands till it completely covered me, then push it forward in the same way when I wanted to get out. As holds for my hands I planted two spikes just where I needed them. These little odds and ends of carpentry, if I may so describe it, carried out with whatever tools and material I chanced to find, gave me a certain pleasure. I knew it would soon be the end, so I played the part, you know, the part of – how shall I say, I don't know. I was comfortable enough in this boat, I must say. The lid fitted so well I had to pierce a hole. It's no good closing your eyes, you must leave them open in the dark, that is my opinion. I am not speaking of sleep, I am speaking of what I believe is called waking. In any case, I slept very little at this period, I wasn't sleepy, or I was too sleepy, I don't know, or I was afraid, I don't know. Flat then on my back I saw nothing except, dimly, just above my head, through the tiny chinks, the grey light of the shed. To see nothing at all, no, that's too much. I heard faintly the cries of the gulls ravening about the mouth of the sewer near by. In a spew of yellow foam, if my memory serves me right, the filth gushed into the river and the slush of birds above screaming with hunger and fury. I heard the lapping of water against the slip and against the bank and the other sound, so different, of open wave, I heard it too. I too, when I moved, felt less boat than wave, or so it seemed to me, and my stillness was the stillness of eddies. That may seem impossible. The rain too, I often heard it, for it often rained. Sometimes a drop, falling through the roof of the shed, exploded on me. All that composed a rather liquid world. And then of course there was the voice of the wind or rather those, so various, of its playthings. But what does it amount to? Howling, soughing, moaning, sighing. What I would have liked was hammer strokes, bang bang bang, clanging in the desert. I let farts to be sure, but hardly ever a real crack, they oozed out with a sucking noise, melted in the mighty never. I don't know how long I stayed there. I was very snug in my box, I must say. It seemed to me I had grown more independent of recent years. That no one came any more, that no one could come any more to ask me if I was all right and needed nothing, distressed me then but little. I was all right, yes, quite so, and the fear of getting worse was less with me. As for my needs, they had dwindled as it were to my dimensions and become, if I may say so, of so exquisite a quality as to exclude all thought of succour. To know I had a being, however faint and false, outside of me, had once had the power to stir my heart. You become unsociable, it's inevitable. It's enough to make you wonder sometimes if you are on the right planet. Even the words desert you, it's as bad as that. Perhaps it's the moment when the vessels stop communicating, you know, the vessels. There you are still between the two murmurs, it must be the same old song as ever, but Christ you wouldn't think so. There were times when I wanted to push away the lid and get out of the boat and couldn't, I was so indolent and weak, so content deep down where I was. I felt them hard upon me, the icy, tumultuous streets, the terrifying faces, the noises that slash, pierce, claw, bruise. So I waited till the desire to shit, or even to piss, lent me wings. I did not want to dirty my nest! And yet it sometimes happened, and even more and more often. Arched and rigid I edged down my trousers and turned a little on my side, just enough to free the hole. To contrive a little kingdom, in the midst of the universal muck, then shit on it, ah that was me all over. The excrements were me too, I know, I know, but all the same. Enough, enough, the next thing I was having visions, I who never did, except sometimes in my sleep, who never had, real visions, I'd remember, except perhaps as a child, my myth will have it so. I knew they were visions because it was night and I was alone in my boat. What else could they have been? So I was in my boat and gliding on the waters. I didn't have to row, the ebb was carrying me out. Anyway I saw no oars, they must have taken them away. I had a board, the remains of a thwart perhaps, which I used when I came too close to the bank, or when a pier came bearing down on me or a barge at its moorings. There were stars in the sky, quite a few. I didn't know what the weather was doing, I was neither cold nor warm and all seemed calm. The banks receded more and more, it was inevitable, soon I saw them no more. The lights grew fainter and fewer as the river widened. There on the land men were sleeping, bodies were gathering strength for the toil and joys of the morrow. The boat was not gliding now, it was tossing, buffeted by the choppy waters of the bay. All seemed calm and yet foam was washing aboard. Now the sea air was all about me, I had no other shelter than the land, and what does it amount to, the shelter of the land, at such a time. I saw the beacons, four in all, including a lightship. I knew them well, even as a child I had known them well. It was evening, I was with my father on a height, he held my

hand. I would have liked him to draw me close with a
gesture of protective love, but his mind was on other
things. He also taught me the names of the mountains.
But to have done with these visions I also saw the lights
of the buoys, the sea seemed full of them, red and green,
and to my surprise even yellow. And on the slopes of the
mountain, now rearing its unbroken bulk behind the
town, the fires turned from gold to red, from red to gold.
I knew what it was, it was the gorse burning. How often
I had set a match to it myself, as a child. And hours later,
back in my home, before I climbed into bed, I watched
from my high window the fires I had lit. That night then,
all aglow with distant fires, on sea, on land and in the sky,
I drifted with the currents and the tides. I noticed that
my hat was tied, with a string I suppose, to my button-
hole. I got up from my seat in the stern and a great
clanking was heard. That was the chain. One end was
fastened to the bow and the other round my waist.
I must have pierced a hole beforehand in the floorboards,
for there I was down on my knees prying out the plug
with my knife. The hole was small and the water rose
slowly. It would take a good half hour, everything
included, barring accidents. Back now in the sternsheets,
my legs stretched out, my back well propped against the
sack stuffed with grass I used as a cushion, I swallowed
my calmative. The sea, the sky, the mountains and the

islands closed in and crushed me in a mighty systole, then scattered to the uttermost confines of space. The memory came faint and cold of the story I might have told, a story in the likeness of my life, I mean without the courage to end or the strength to go on.

Translated by Richard Seaver in collaboration with the author

The Calmative

I don't know when I died. It always seemed to me I died old, about ninety years old, and what years, and that my body bore it out, from head to foot. But this evening, alone in my icy bed, I have the feeling I'll be older than the day, the night, when the sky with all its lights fell upon me, the same I had so often gazed on since my first stumblings on the distant earth. For I'm too frightened this evening to listen to myself rot, waiting for the great red lapses of the heart, the tearings at the caecal walls, and for the slow killings to finish in my skull, the assaults on unshakable pillars, the fornications with corpses. So I'll tell myself a story, I'll try and tell myself another story, to try and calm myself, and it's there I feel I'll be old, old, even older than the day I fell, calling for help, and it came. Or is it possible that in this story I have come back to life, after my death? No, it's not like me to come back to life, after my death.

What possessed me to stir when I wasn't with any-body? Was I being thrown out? No, I wasn't with any-body. I see a kind of den littered with empty tins. And yet we are not in the country. Perhaps it's just ruins, a ruined folly, on the skirts of the town, in a field, for the fields come right up to our walls, their walls, and the cows lie down at night in the lee of the ramparts. I have changed refuge so often, in the course of my rout, that now I can't tell between dens and ruins. But there was never any city but the one. It is true you often move along in a dream, houses and factories darken the air, trams go by and under your feet wet from the grass there are suddenly cobbles. I only know the city of my childhood, I must have seen the other, but unbelieving. All I say cancels out, I'll have said nothing. Was I hungry itself? Did the weather tempt me? It was cloudy and cool, I insist, but not to the extent of luring me out. I couldn't get up at the first attempt, nor let us say at the second, and once up, propped against the wall, I wondered if I could go on, I mean up, propped against the wall. Impossible to go out and walk. I speak as though it all happened yesterday. Yesterday indeed is recent, but not enough. For what I tell this evening is passing this evening, at this passing hour. I'm no longer with these assassins, in this bed of terror, but in my distant refuge, my hands twined together, my head bowed, weak, breathless, calm, free, and older than I'll have ever been, if my calculations are correct. I'll tell my story in the past none the less, as though it were a myth, or an old fable, for this evening I need another age, that age to become another age in which I became what I was.

But little by little I got myself out and started walking with short steps among the trees, oh look, trees! The paths of other days were rank with tangled growth. I leaned against the trunks to get my breath and pulled myself forward with the help of boughs. Of my last passage no trace remained. They were the perishing oaks immortalized by d'Aubigné. It was only a grove. The fringe was near, a light less green and kind of tattered told me so, in a whisper. Yes, no matter where you stood, in this little wood, and were it in the furthest recess of its poor secrecies, you saw on every hand the gleam of this pale light, promise of God knows what fatuous eternity. Die without too much pain, a little, that's worth your while. Under the blind sky close with your own hands the eyes soon sockets, then quick into carrion not to mislead the crows. That's the advantage of death by drowning, one of the advantages, the crabs never get there too soon. But here a strange thing, I was no sooner free of the wood at last, having crossed unminding the ditch that girdles it, than thoughts came to me of cruelty, the kind that smiles. A lush pasture lay before me, nonsuch perhaps, who cares, drenched in evening dew or recent rain. Beyond this meadow to my certain knowledge a path, then a field and finally the ramparts, closing the prospect. Cyclopean and crenellated, standing out faintly against a sky scarcely less sombre, they did not seem in ruins, viewed from mine, but were, to my certain knowledge. Such was the scene offered to me, in vain, for I knew it well and loathed it. What I saw was a bald man in a brown suit, a comedian. He was telling a funny story about a fiasco. Its point escaped me. He used the word snail, or slug, to the delight of all present. The women seemed even more entertained than their escorts, if that were possible. Their shrill laughter pierced the clapping and, when this had subsided, broke out still here and there in sudden peals even after the next story had begun, so that part of it was lost. Perhaps they had in mind the reigning penis sitting who knows by their side and from that sweet shore launched their cries of joy towards the comic vast, what a talent. But it's to me this evening something has to happen, to my body as in myth and metamorphosis, this old body to which nothing ever happened, or so little, which never met with anything, loved anything, wished for anything, in its tarnished universe, except for the mirrors to shatter, the plane, the curved, the magnifying, the minifying, and to vanish in the havoc of its images. Yes, this evening it has to be as in the story my father used to read to me, evening after evening, when I was small, and he had all his health, to calm me, evening after evening, year after year it seems to me this evening, which I don't remember much about, except that it was the adventures of one Joe Breem, or Breen, the son of a lighthouse keeper, a strong muscular lad of fifteen, those were the words, who swam for miles in the night, a knife between his teeth, after a shark, I forget why, out of sheer heroism. He might have simply told me the story, he knew it by heart, so did I, but that wouldn't have calmed me, he had to read it to me, evening after evening, or pretend to read it to me, turning the pages and explaining the pictures that were of me already, evening after evening the same pictures till I dozed off on his shoulder. If he had skipped a single word I would have hit him, with my little fist, in his big belly bursting out of the old cardigan and unbuttoned trousers that rested him from his office canonicals. For me now the setting forth, the struggle and perhaps the return, for the old man I am this evening, older than my father ever was, older than I shall ever be. I crossed the meadow with little stiff steps at the same time limp, the best I could manage. Of my last passage no trace remained, it was long ago. And the little bruised stems soon straighten up again, having need of air and light, and as for the broken their place is soon taken. I entered the town by what they call the Shepherds' Gate without having seen a soul, only the first bats like flying crucifixions, nor heard a sound except my steps, my heart in my breast and then, as I went under the arch, the hoot of an owl, that cry at once so soft and fierce which in the night, calling, answering, through my little wood and those nearby, sounded in my shelter like a tocsin. The further I went into the city the more I was struck by its deserted air. It was lit as usual, brighter than usual, although the shops were shut. But the lights were on in their windows with the object no doubt of attracting customers and prompting them to say, I say, I like that, not dear either, I'll come back tomorrow, if I'm still alive. I nearly said, Good God it's Sunday. The trams were running, the buses too, but few, slow, empty, noiseless, as if under water. I didn't see a single horse! I was wearing my long green greatcoat with the velvet collar, such as motorists wore about 1900, my father's, but that day it was sleeveless, a vast cloak. But on me it was still the same great dead weight, with no warmth to it, and the tails swept the ground, scraped it rather, they had grown so stiff, and I so shrunken. What would, what could happen to me in this empty place? But I felt the houses packed with people, lurking behind the curtains they looked out into the street or, crouched far back in the depths of the room, head in hands, were sunk in dream. Up aloft my hat, the same as always, I reached no further. I went right across the city and came to the sea, having followed the river to its mouth. I kept saying, I'll go back,

unbelieving. The boats at anchor in the harbour, tied up
to the jetty, seemed no less numerous than usual, as if I
knew anything about what was usual. But the quays were
deserted and there was no sign or stir of arrival or depart-
ure. But all might change from one moment to the next
and be transformed like magic before my eyes. Then all
the bustle of the people and things of the sea, the masts
of the big craft gravely rocking and of the small more
jauntily, I insist, and I'd hear the gulls' terrible cry and
perhaps the sailors' cry. And I might slip unnoticed
aboard a freighter outward bound and get far away and
spend far away a few good months, perhaps even a year
or two, in the sun, in peace, before I died. And without
going that far it would be a sad state of affairs if in that
unscandalizable throng I couldn't achieve a little encoun-
ter that would calm me a little, or exchange a few words
with a navigator for example, words to carry away with
me to my refuge, to add to my collection. I waited sitting
on a kind of topless capstan, saying, The very capstans
this evening are out of order. And I gazed out to sea, out
beyond the breakwaters, without sighting the least ves-
sel. I could see lights flush with the water. And the pretty
beacons at the harbour mouth I could see too, and others
in the distance, flashing from the coast, the islands, the
headlands. But seeing still no sign or stir I made ready to
go, to turn away sadly from this dead haven, for there are

scenes that call for strange farewells. I had merely to bow
my head and look down at my feet, for it is in this attitude
I always drew the strength to, how shall I say, I don't
know, and it was always from the earth, rather than from
the sky, notwithstanding its reputation, that my help
came in time of trouble. And there, on the flagstone,
which I was not focusing, for why focus it, I saw haven
afar, where the black swell was most perilous, and all
about me storm and wreck. I'll never come back here,
I said. But when with a thrust of both hands against the
the rim of the capstan I heaved myself up I found facing
me a young boy holding a goat by a horn. I sat down
again. He stood there silent looking at me without visible
fear or revulsion. Admittedly the light was poor. His
silence seemed natural to me, it befitted me as the elder
to speak first. He was barefoot and in rags. Haunter of
the waterfront he had stepped aside to see what the dark
hulk could be abandoned on the quayside. Such was my
train of thought. Close up to me now with his little gut-
tersnipe's eye there could be no doubt left in his mind.
And yet he stayed. Can this base thought be mine?
Moved, for after all that is what I must have come out for,
in a way, and with little expectation of advantage from
what might follow, I resolved to speak to him. So I mar-
shalled the words and opened my mouth, thinking I
would hear them. But all I heard was a kind of rattle,

unintelligible even to me who knew what was intended. But it was nothing, mere speechlessness due to long silence, as in the wood that darkens the mouth of hell, do you remember, I only just. Without letting go of his goat he moved right up against me and offered me a sweet out of a twist of paper such as you could buy for a penny. I hadn't been offered a sweet for eighty years at least, but I took it eagerly and put it in my mouth, the old gesture came back to me, more and more moved since that is what I wanted. The sweets were stuck together and I had my work cut out to separate the top one, a green one, from the others, but he helped me and his hand brushed mine. And a moment later as he made to move away, hauling his goat after him, with a great gesticulation of my whole body I motioned him to stay and I said, in an impetuous murmur, Where are you off to, my little man, with your nanny? The words were hardly out of my mouth when for shame I covered my face. And yet they were the same I had tried to utter but a moment before. Where are you off to, my little man, with your nanny! If I could have blushed I would have, but there was not enough blood left in my extremities. If I had had a penny in my pocket I would have given it to him, for him to forgive me, but I did not have a penny in my pocket, nor anything resembling it. Nothing that could give pleasure to a little unfortunate at the mouth of life.

I suspect I had nothing with me but my stone, that day, having gone out as it were without premeditation. Of his little person I was fated to see no more than the black curly hair and the pretty curve of the long bare legs all muscle and dirt. And the hand, so fresh and keen, I would not forget in a hurry either. I looked for better words to say to him, I found them too late, he was gone, oh not far, but far. Out of my life too he went without a care, not one of his thoughts would ever be for me again, unless perhaps when he was old and, delving in his boyhood, would come upon that gallows night and hold the goat by the horn again and linger again a moment by my side, with who knows perhaps a touch of tenderness, even of envy, but I have my doubts. Poor dear dumb beasts, how you will have helped me. What does your daddy do? that's what I would have said to him if he had given me the chance. Soon they were no more than a single blur which if I hadn't known I might have taken for a young centaur. I was nearly going to have the goat dung, then pick up a handful of the pellets so soon cold and hard, sniff and even taste them, no, that would not help me this evening. I say this evening as if it were always the same evening, but are there two evenings? I went, intending to get back as fast as I could, but it would not be quite empty-handed, repeating, I'll never come back here. My legs were paining me, every step would gladly have been the last, but the glances I darted towards the windows, stealthily, showed me a great cylinder sweeping past as though on rollers on the asphalt. I must indeed have been moving fast, for I overhauled more than one pedestrian, there are the first men, without extending myself, I who in the normal way was left standing by cripples, and then I seemed to hear the footfalls die behind me. And yet each little step would gladly have been the last. So much so that when I emerged on a square I hadn't noticed on the way out, with a cathedral looming on the far side, I decided to go in, if it was open, and hide, as in the Middle Ages, for a space. I say cathedral, it may not have been, I don't know, all I know is it would vex me in this story that aspires to be the last, to have taken refuge in a common church. I remarked the Saxon Stützenwechsel. Charming effect, but it didn't charm me. The brilliantly lit nave appeared deserted. I walked round it several times without seeing a soul. They were hiding perhaps, under the choir stalls, or dodging behind the pillars, like woodpeckers. Suddenly close to where I was, and without my having heard the long preliminary rumblings, the organ began to boom. I sprang up from the mat on which I lay before the altar and hastened to the far end of the nave as if on my way out. But it was a side aisle and the door I disappeared through was not the exit. For instead of being restored to the night

43

I found myself at the foot of a spiral staircase which I began to climb at top speed, mindless of my heart, like one hotly pursued by a homicidal maniac. This staircase faintly lit by I know not what means, slits perhaps, I mounted panting as far as the projecting gallery in which it culminated and which, separated from the void by a cynical parapet, encompassed a smooth round wall capped by a little dome covered with lead or verdigrised copper, phew, if that's not clear. People must have come here for the view, those who fall die on the way. Flattening myself against the wall I started round, clockwise. But I had hardly gone a few steps when I met a man revolving in the other direction, with the utmost circumspection. How I'd love to push him, or him to push me, over the edge. He gazed at me wild-eyed for a moment and then, not daring to pass me on the parapet side and surmising correctly that I would not relinquish the wall just to oblige him, abruptly turned his back on me, his head rather, for his back remained glued to the wall, and went back the way he had come so that soon there was nothing left of him but a left hand. It lingered a moment, then slid out of sight. All that remained to me was the vision of two burning eyes starting out of their sockets under a check cap. Into what nightmare thingness am I fallen? My hat flew off, but did not get far thanks to the string. I turned my head towards the staircase and lent

an eye. Nothing. Then a little girl came into view followed by a man holding her by the hand, both pressed
against the wall. He pushed her into the stairway, disappeared after her, turned and raised towards me a face that
made me recoil. I could only see his bare head above the
top step. When they were gone I called. I completed in
haste the round of the gallery. No one. I saw on the horizon, where sky, sea, plain and mountain meet, a few low
stars, not to be confused with the fires men light, at night,
or that go alight alone. Enough. Back in the street I tried
to find my way in the sky, where I knew the Bears so well.
If I had seen someone I would have stopped him to ask,
the most ferocious aspect would not have daunted me.
I would have said, touching my hat, Pardon me your honour, the Shepherds' Gate for the love of God. I thought I
could go no further, but no sooner had the impetus
reached my legs than on I went, believe it or not, at a very
fair pace. I wasn't returning empty-handed, not quite,
I was taking back with me the virtual certainty that I was
still of this world, of that world too, in a way. But I was
paying the price. I would have done better to spend the
night in the cathedral, on the mat before the altar,
I would have continued on my way at first light, or they
would have found me stretched out in the rigor of death,
the genuine bodily article, under the blue eyes fount of
so much hope, and put me in the evening papers. But

suddenly I was descending a wide street, vaguely familiar, but in which I could never have set foot, in my lifetime. But soon realizing I was going downhill I turned about and set off in the other direction. For I was afraid if I went downhill of returning to the sea where I had sworn never to return. When I say I turned about I mean I wheeled round in a wide semicircle without slowing down, for I was afraid if I stopped of not being able to start again, yes, I was afraid of that too. And this evening too I dare not stop. I was struck more and more by the contrast between the brightly lit streets and their deserted air. To say it distressed me, no, but I say it all the same, in the hope of calming myself. To say there was no one abroad, no, I would not go that far, for I remarked a number of shapes, male and female, strange shapes, but not more so than usual. As to what hour it might have been I had no idea, except that it must have been some hour of the night. But it might have been three or four in the morning just as it might have been ten or eleven in the evening, depending no doubt on whether one wondered at the scarcity of passers-by or at the extraordinary radiance shed by the street lamps and traffic lights. For at one or other of these no one could fail to wonder, unless he was out of his mind. Not a single private car but admittedly from time to time a public vehicle, slow sweep of light silent and empty. It is not my wish to labour these antinomies, for we are needless to say in a skull, but I have no choice but to add the following few remarks. All the mortals I saw were alone and as if sunk in themselves. It must be a common sight but mixed with something else I imagine. The only couple was two men grappling, their legs intertwined. I only saw one cyclist! He was going the same way as I was. All were going the same way as I was, vehicles too, I have only just realized it. He was pedalling slowly in the middle of the street, reading a newspaper which he held with both hands spread open before his eyes. Every now and then he rang his bell without interrupting his reading. I watched him recede till he was no more than a dot on the horizon. Suddenly a young woman perhaps of easy virtue, dishevelled and her dress in disarray, darted across the street like a rabbit. That is all I had to add. But here a strange thing, yet another, I had no pain whatever, not even in my legs. Weakness. A good night's nightmare and a tin of sardines would restore my sensitivity. My shadow, one of my shadows, flew before me, dwindled, slid under my feet, trailed behind me the way shadows will. This degree of opacity appeared to me conclusive. But suddenly ahead of me a man on the same side of the street and going the same way, to keep harping on the same thing lest I forget. The distance between us was considerable, seventy paces at least, and fearing he might escape me I quickened my step with the result I swept forward as if on rollers. This is not me, I said, let us make the most of it. Finding myself in an instant a bare ten paces in his rear I slowed down so as not to burst in on him and so heighten the aversion my person inspired even in its most abject and obsequious attitudes. And a moment later, keeping humbly in step with him, Excuse me your honour, the Shepherds' Gate for the love of God! At close quarters he appeared normal apart from that air already noted of ebbing inward. I drew a few steps ahead, turned, cringed, touched my hat and said, The right time for mercy's sake! I might as well not have existed. But what about the sweet? A light! I cried. Given my need of help I can't think why I did not bar his path. I couldn't have, that's all, I couldn't have touched him. Seeing a stone seat by the kerb I sat down and crossed my legs, like Walther. I must have dozed off, for the next thing was a man sitting beside me. I was still taking him in when he opened his eyes and set them on me, as if for the first time, for he shrank back unaffectedly. Where did you spring from? he said. To hear myself addressed again so soon impressed me greatly. What's the matter with you? he said. I tried to look like one with whom that only is the matter which is native to him. Forgive me your honour, I said, gingerly lifting my hat and rising a fraction from the seat, the right time for the love of God! He said a time, I don't remem-

ber which, a time that explained nothing, that's all
I remember, and did not calm me. But what time could
have done that? Oh I know, I know, one will come that
will. But in the meantime? What's that you said? he said.
Unfortunately I had said nothing. But I wriggled out of
it by asking him if he could help me find my way which
I had lost. No, he said, for I am not from these parts
and if I am sitting on this slab it is because the hotels
were full or would not let me in, I have no opinion. But
tell me the story of your life, then we'll see. My life! I
cried. Why yes, he said, you know, that kind of – what
shall I say? He brooded for a time, no doubt trying to
think of what life could well be said to be a kind. In the
end he went on, testily, Come now, everyone knows that.
He jogged me in the ribs. No details, he said, the main
drift, the main drift. But as I remained silent he said, Shall
I tell you mine, then you'll see what I mean. The account
he then gave was brief and dense, facts, without com-
ment. That's what I call a life, he said, do you follow me
now? It wasn't bad, his story, positively fairy-like in places.
But that Pauline, I said, are you still with her? I am, he
said, but I'm going to leave her and set up with another,
younger and plumper. You travel a lot, I said. Oh widely,
widely, he said. Words were coming back to me, and the
way to make them sound. All that's a thing of the past
for you no doubt, he said. Do you think of spending

some time among us? I said. This sentence struck me as particularly well turned. If it's not a rude question, he said, how old are you? I don't know, I said. You don't know! he cried. Not exactly, I said. Are thighs much in your thoughts, he said, arses, cunts and environs? I didn't follow. No more erections naturally, he said. Erections? I said. The penis, he said, you know what the penis is, there, between the legs. Ah that! I said. It thickens, lengthens, stiffens and rises, he said, does it not? I assented, though they were not the terms I would have used. That is what we call an erection, he said. He pondered, then exclaimed, Phenomenal! No? Strange right enough, I said. And there you have it all, he said. But what will become of her? I said. Who? he said. Pauline, I said. She will grow old, he said with tranquil assurance, slowly at first, then faster and faster, in pain and bitterness, pulling the devil by the tail. The face was not full, but I eyed it in vain, it remained clothed in its flesh instead of turning all chalky and channelled as with a gouge. The very vomer kept its cushion. It is true discussion was always bad for me. I longed for the tender nonsuch, I would have trodden it gently, with my boots in my hand, and for the shade of my wood, far from this terrible light. What are you grinning and bearing? he said. He held on his knees a big black bag, like a midwife's I imagine. It was full of glittering phials. I asked him if they were all alike. Oho

no, he said, for every taste. He took one and held it out
to me, saying, One and six. What did he want? To sell it
to me? Proceeding on this hypothesis I told him I had no
money. No money! he cried. All of a sudden his hand
came down on the back of my neck, his sinewy fingers
closed and with a jerk and a twist he had me up against
him. But instead of dispatching me he began to murmur
words so sweet that I went limp and my head fell forward
in his lap. Between the caressing voice and the fingers
rowelling my neck the contrast was striking. But grad-
ually the two things merged in a devastating hope, if I
dare say so, and I dare. For this evening I have nothing to
lose that I can discern. And if I have reached this point
(in my story) without anything having changed, for if
anything had changed I think I'd know, the fact remains
I have reached it, and that's something, and with nothing
changed, and that's something too. It's no excuse for
rushing matters. No, it must cease gently, as gently cease
on the stairs the steps of the loved one, who could not
love and will not come back, and whose steps say so, that
she could not love and will not come back. He suddenly
shoved me away and showed me the phial again. There
you have it all, he said. It can't have been the same all as
before. Want it? he said. No, but I said yes, so as not to
vex him. He proposed an exchange. Give me your hat, he
said. I refused. What vehemence! he said. I haven't a

thing, I said. Try in your pockets, he said. I haven't a thing, I said, I came out without a thing. Give me a lace, he said. I refused. Long silence. And if you gave me a kiss, he said finally. I knew there were kisses in the air. Can you take off your hat? he said. I took it off. Put it back, he said, you look nicer with it on. I put it back. Come on, he said, give me a kiss and let there be an end to it. Did it not occur to him I might turn him down? No, a kiss is not a bootlace, he must have seen from my face that all passion was not quite spent. Come, he said. I wiped my mouth in its tod of hair and advanced it towards his. Just a moment, he said. My mouth stood still. You know what a kiss is? he said. Yes yes, I said. If it's not a rude question, he said, when was your last? Some time ago, I said, but I can still do them. He took off his hat, a bowler, and tapped the middle of his forehead. There, he said, and there only. He had a noble brow, white and high. He leaned forward, closing his eyes. Quick, he said. I pursed up my lips as mother had taught me and brought them down where he had said. Enough, he said. He raised his hand to the spot, but left the gesture unfinished and put on his hat. I turned away and looked across the street. It was then I noticed we were sitting opposite a horse-butcher's. Here, he said, take it. I had forgotten. He rose. Standing he was quite short. One good turn, he said, with radiant smile. His teeth shone. I listened to his steps

die away. How tell what remains? But it's the end. Or
have I been dreaming, am I dreaming? No no, none of
that, for dream is nothing, a joke, and significant what is
worse. I said, Stay where you are till day breaks, wait
sleeping till the lamps go out and the streets come to life.
But I stood up and moved off. My pains were back, but
with something untoward which prevented my wrap-
ping them round me. But I said, Little by little you are
coming to. From my gait alone, slow, stiff and which
seemed at every step to solve a statodynamic problem
never posed before, I would have been known again, if I
had been known. I crossed over and stopped before the
butcher's. Behind the grille the curtains were drawn,
rough canvas curtains striped blue and white, colours of
the Virgin, and stained with great pink stains. They did
not quite meet in the middle, and through the chink I
could make out the dim carcasses of the gutted horses
hanging from hooks head downwards. I hugged the
walls, famished for shadow. To think that in a moment
all will be said, all to do again. And the city clocks, what
was wrong with them, whose great chill clang even in
my wood fell on me from the air? What else? Ah yes, my
spoils. I tried to think of Pauline, but she eluded me,
gleamed an instant and was gone, like the young woman
in the street. So I went in the atrocious brightness, bed-
ded in my old flesh, straining towards an issue and

passing them by to left and right and my mind panting after this and that and always flung back to where there was nothing. I succeeded however in fastening briefly on the little girl, long enough to see her a little more clearly than before, so that she wore a kind of bonnet and clasped in her hand a book, of common prayer perhaps, and to try and have her smile, but she did not smile, but vanished down the staircase without having yielded me her little face. I had to stop. At first nothing, then little by little, I mean rising up out of the silence till suddenly no higher, a kind of massive murmur coming perhaps from the house that was propping me up. That reminded me that the houses were full of people, besieged, no, I don't know. When I stepped back to look at the windows I could see, in spite of shutters, blinds and muslins, that many of the rooms were lit. The light was so dimmed by the brilliancy flooding the boulevard that short of knowing or suspecting it was not so one might have supposed everyone sleeping. The sound was not continuous, but broken by silences possibly of consternation. I thought of ringing at the door and asking for shelter and protection till morning. But suddenly I was on my way again. But little by little, in a slow swoon, darkness fell about me. I saw a mass of bright flowers fade in an exquisite cascade of paling colours. I found myself admiring, all along the housefronts, the gradual blossoming of squares and rectangles casement and sash, yellow, green, pink, according to the curtains and blinds, finding that pretty. Then at last, before I fell, first to my knees, as cattle do, then on my face, I was in a throng. I didn't lose consciousness, when I lose consciousness it will not be to recover it. They paid no heed to me, though careful not to walk on me, a courtesy that must have touched me, it was what I had come out for. It was well with me, sated with dark and calm, lying at the feet of mortals, fathom deep in the grey of dawn, if it was dawn. But reality, too tired to look for the right word, was soon restored, the throng fell away, the light came back and I had no need to raise my head from the ground to know I was back in the same blinding void as before. I said, Stay where you are, down on the friendly stone, or at least indifferent, don't open your eyes, wait for morning. But up with me again and back on the way that was not mine, on uphill along the boulevard. A blessing he was not waiting for me, poor old Breem, or Breen. I said, The sea is east, it's west I must go, to the left of north. But in vain I raised without hope my eyes to the sky to look for the Bears. For the light I steeped in put out the stars, assuming they were there, which I doubted, remembering the clouds.

Translated by the author

SAMUEL BECKETT

The End

Translated by
Samuel Beckett and Richard Seaver

PENGUIN BOOKS

PENGUIN CLASSICS

UK | USA | Canada | Ireland | Australia
India | New Zealand | South Africa

Penguin Books is part of the Penguin Random House group
of companies whose addresses can be found at
global.penguinrandomhouse.com.

Penguin
Random House
UK

This selection first published 2018
001

Set in 11.2/13.75 pt Dante MT Std
Typeset by Jouve (UK), Milton Keynes
Printed in Great Britain by Clays Ltd, St Ives plc

ISBN: 978–0–241–33897–1

www.greenpenguin.co.uk

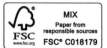